# The ART COLLECTOR

Jan Wahl          Illustrated by Rosalinde Bonnet

ini Charlesbridge

For Jeff Grove, artist and friend—J. W.

For Umberto and Sofia—R. B.

Text copyright © 2011 by Jan Wahl
Illustrations copyright © 2011 by Rosalinde Bonnet
All rights reserved, including the right of reproduction in whole or in part in
any form. Charlesbridge and colophon are registered trademarks of Charlesbridge
Publishing, Inc.

Published by Charlesbridge
85 Main Street
Watertown, MA 02472
(617) 926-0329
www.charlesbridge.com

**Library of Congress Cataloging-in-Publication Data**
Wahl, Jan.
    The art collector / Jan Wahl ; illustrated by Rosalinde Bonnet.
        p. cm.
    Summary: A little boy who is not pleased with his own artistic efforts
but treasures his great-grandmother's drawing goes on to collect art throughout
his life.
    ISBN 978-1-58089-270-4 (reinforced for library use)
    [1. Art—Collectors and collecting—Fiction.]  I. Bonnet, Rosalinde, ill.
II. Title.
PZ7.W1266Art 2011
[E]—dc22                2010022760

Printed in China
(hc) 10 9 8 7 6 5 4 3 2 1

Illustrations done in acrylic paint, pencil, and collage on acrylic special paper
    Clairefontaine (165 lb.)
Text type set in Goudy
Color separations by Chroma Graphics, Singapore
Printed and bound February 2011 by Jade Productions in Heyuan Province,
    Guangdong, China
Production supervision by Brian G. Walker
Designed by Susan Mallory Sherman

When Oscar was very, very, very small,
Great-Granny took a piece of paper.

Then she took a crayon,
and began making lines.

Some were straight.

Some were curving.

Soon, in a minute or two, it was not a blank piece of paper.

It was a chicken. It was magic.
Oscar watched, and clapped his hands.

"Can I do it?" he asked.

"You can try," said Great-Granny.

And she handed him the crayon.

Oscar made many lines, short and long,

on another piece of paper.

The crayon slid, swirled, and danced.

What he made was not a chicken.
In fact, it didn't look like anything.
Oscar frowned.
And he crumpled it up.

Great-Granny handed him
a sheet of black paper
and a stick of white chalk.
"Try again," she said.

The stick of chalk hopped all over
the sheet of black paper.
Oscar was about to tear it up.
"I still don't have a chicken,"
he grumbled.

grrrrr

Great-Granny looked carefully with her good eye.
Then she put on her glasses,
and held the paper this way.
And that way.

"You have made
a very fine picture
of a snowstorm
on a very dark night."

Ma and Pa framed it—
and hung it for visitors to admire.
They also framed Great-Granny's red chicken.
Some people preferred the snow scene.
Many liked both.

Great-Granny's visit was over.
But Oscar kept the chicken.
He thought her drawing was better than his.
And he liked looking at it.

Oscar liked to go with his parents
to Sunday shows, where artists
sold pictures.
They took him to flea markets, too.

Oscar found an old etching
in a beat-up frame.
It was a stream with a building
and a waterwheel.
Oscar heard the sound of water turning the wheel.

The etching cost one dollar.

Oscar counted out coins and tugged at Pa.

"I must have it," he said.

"Will you lend me the rest?"

"I'll pull out weeds
and help Ma, too."

OSCAR HAD BOUGHT HIS FIRST PICTURE.

After taking it home and dusting it off,
he saw the glass had a crack.

So they took the etching of a stream
and a building and a waterwheel
to the framer's.

The new frame and glass, better backing,
and wire to hang it cost
more than the picture.
Oscar had to pull many, many weeds.

But he could see the picture a lot better.
And he liked looking at it.

Slowly the years passed.
Oscar grew taller. He kept collecting
until pictures hung
on every wall of his room.

In one painting, four geese HONKED.

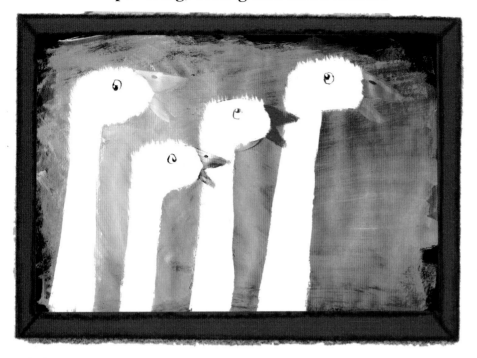

In a Japanese woodcut,
a bamboo lute STRUMMED
under a round moon.

In one drawing, leaves WHISTLED
in the wild, wild wind.

In some, just plain colors
SANG—in circles . . .

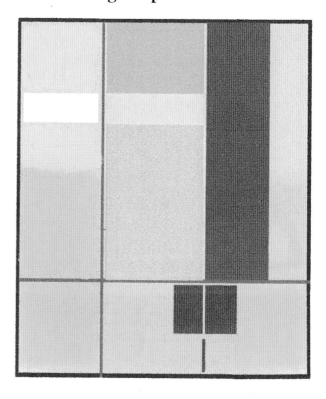

and oblong shapes . . .

and puffs of color.

And as Oscar looked,
the pictures changed in front of him.
Now a forest had more trees.

Yesterday that lady
wore a pink hat.
Today it was yellow.
Or was it purple?
Orange? Magenta?

At night, before turning off
the lamp, he waved at his pictures.
The room became quiet
and the pictures slept, too.

And when he grew up and moved away,
Oscar packed them all—
wrapping each one
in thick brown paper so it wouldn't break.

He loved his pictures.
Every one.

The years passed.
And his collection became famous.
Newspapers wrote about it.
Oscar's collection grew
and g r e w
and G R E W—

until a museum had to be built to hold it.

Oscar kept one picture for himself.
And he loved looking at it.